Ms. Bitsy Bat's Kindergarten

by Pamela Duncan Edwards illustrated by Henry Cole

HYPERION BOOKS FOR CHILDREN

NEW YORK

This book is for my little friends, Britt and Ben Osborne, with love
—P.D.E.

For Dot Patterson, a wonderful third grade teacher
—H.C.

Text copyright © 2005 by Pamela Duncan Edwards
Illustrations copyright © 2005 by Henry Cole
Hand lettering by Leah Palmer Preiss
Design by Elizabeth Clark

Printed in Singapore
First Edition
1 3 5 7 9 10 8 6 4 2

ISBN 0-7868-0669-9
This book is set in Caslon Antique.
Library of Congress Cataloging-in-Publication Data on file.
Reinforced binding
Visit www.hyperionbooksforchildren.com

It was the second day of the new year at Oak Tree School.

"Strange," said Possum, "I thought Mr. Fox would be here to welcome us again."

"Isn't he?" asked Mole. "I can't see. I've lost my glasses."

Just then, they heard a patter of feet behind them.

"News!" squeaked Mouse importantly. "I was the very first to hear it. Mrs. Fox had five babies last night. Mr. Fox has to stay home to help her. We're going to have a new teacher and a new classroom!"

"A NEW TEACHER!" cried everyone. "But Mr. Fox was our teacher yesterday."

Mr. Fox said having me in his class was interesting. I bet this new teacher won't even know how smart I am.

Mr. Fox smiled a lot. I bet this new teacher will be a grouch.

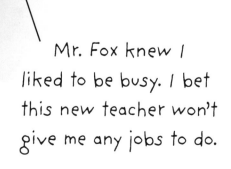

Mr. Fox knew I liked to be busy. I bet this new teacher won't give me any jobs to do.

Mr. Fox understood all about my allergies. I bet this new teacher won't have dusted the classroom.

Mr. Fox knew where to find my glasses. I bet this new teacher won't be a good glasses-finder.

Mr. Fox gave us chocolate-chip cookies for snacks. I bet this new teacher will give us yucky carrot sticks.

"What if this new teacher is mean?" they groaned.

"I guess we'd better go in," said Possum, pushing open the classroom door.

"Hey," he said. "There's no one here."

"Oh, no!" squealed Mouse. "Call the police! Somebody's stolen the teacher."

"Just a minute," whispered Rabbit.
"What's that hanging from the ceiling?
It's breathing!"

Suddenly the thing stretched
its wings and glided gracefully
down to the desk.

"Hello," it said. "I'm your
new teacher."

"But you can't be," cried Rabbit. "You're a BAT! My uncle Lop told me bats sleep in the daytime."

"Uncle Lop is right," said the bat with a big yawn. "But I heard that you needed me, so here I am. I'm Ms. Bitsy Bat, and I'm very pleased to have you in my class."

"This is going to be worse than we thought," whispered Groundhog to Mole. "I bet she'll give us slugs for snacks."

"Now that we've met," said Bitsy Bat, "shall we all sit down?"

My tail doesn't fit.

I can't see the board from here. I don't know where my glasses are.

There isn't *any* of me that fits. The desk is too small.

Possum sat down at the teacher's desk.

Bitsy Bat clapped her wings. "What a mix-up," she said. "Possum, dear, this is my desk."

"But you're new," replied Possum. "I thought you might need help."

"How about keeping an eye on things from the back of the room?" suggested Ms. Bat.

"Right! Good idea!" agreed Possum.

"What about me?" asked Mole. "I can't see because I've lost my glasses."

Bitsy Bat lifted Mole's glasses off his head, propped them on his nose, and pulled his desk forward. "You'll be able to see from here," she said.

"Wow!" said Mole admiringly.

"You're a great glasses-finder, Ms. Bat."

Bitsy Bat smiled at Snake. "Why don't you sit at the tall, thin desk so that Groundhog can have the short, wide one?"

"That's pretty clever," whispered Snake.

"Humph!" snorted Groundhog. "I still don't want slugs for snacks!"

"Groundhog," said Ms. Bat, "you're nearest to the snack shelf. Would you be in charge of it for us?"

A big smile spread over Groundhog's face.

"Mouse," said Bitsy Bat, "will you sit by the supply cupboard and give out the pencils each day?"

"Oooo!" squeaked Mouse. "That would keep me very busy."

"If that's my desk by the window," said Rabbit, "my ears will get too hot. I have very sensitive ears, you know."

"We could open the window to cool off your ears," suggested Bitsy Bat.

"Okay," agreed Rabbit. But as he pushed up the sash, something buzzed through the open window.

"Get out!" screamed Rabbit.

"Who?" said Mole. "Who are you talking to?"

"Put your glasses back on," squeaked Mouse. "There's a BEE in our classroom!"

"Is it dangerous?" hissed Snake.

"I'll look it up in the animal encyclopedia," cried Possum. "How do you spell 'bee'?"

"Save the snacks!" yelled Groundhog.

The bee began to buzz around Rabbit's ears with a naughty grin on its face.

"Oh! Oh!" cried Rabbit. "I'm allergic to bee germs!"

Suddenly Bitsy Bat launched herself into the air.

"Duck!" cried Possum.

"Wow!" gasped Snake. "She flies faster than sound!"

The terrified bee raced back out the window, pursued by Bitsy Bat.

A few moments later Ms. Bat flew back into the room.

"I spoke to Bee," she said. "You needn't worry about him anymore."

"We won't," said Rabbit. "Not with you to look after us."

Bitsy Bat laughed. "Groundhog, fetch the snacks.
I think we deserve a treat."

"I don't like slugs, you know, Ms. Bat," said Groundhog anxiously, as he picked up the tin. "I don't like carrot sticks either."

But when Groundhog opened the lid he gave a cry.

"CHOCOLATE-CHIP COOKIES!"

"This is a yummy day at school," sang everyone. "You're a great teacher, Ms. Bat,"

"I think so, too," said Bee.